Sammie's Flat Dog

# Sammie's Flat Dog

Written and Illustrated by

## Gary Alan Shockley

the pilgrim press

The Pilgrim Press, 700 Prospect Avenue East
Cleveland, Ohio 44115-1100
thepilgrimpress.com

Published 2022.

Printed on acid-free paper.

26 25 24 23 22      1 2 3 4 5

Library of Congress Cataloging-in-Publication Data on file.
LCCN: 2021948745

ISBN 978-0-8298-0002-9 (hardcover)

Printed in The United States of America.

To all the pets that have filled our lives with love and joy.
And to my sweet little Zoe.

Sammie wanted a dog more than anything else.

More than ice cream with rainbow sprinkles. More than watching scary movies. More than holding hands with her buddy, Sarah Jane. A million times more!

Mama Carla said Sammie was too young to take care of a dog. Mama Stacy said their house was too small. Sammie didn't care about any of that. She just wanted a dog of her very own.

Sammie sat on the floor by her bed looking at pictures in her favorite dog book. "If they won't get me a dog, I'll make my own!" Sammie said to herself. And just like that she came up with a wonderful plan.

Sammie looked at each picture until she saw the right one. "Perfect," she said pointing at a page. "This one will be great!"

Carefully, Sammie tore the page from her book "Ripppp...." and then held the picture in her hands. "You'll be my Flat Dog!" Sammie said with a heart full of joy. "We'll run and play and have lots of fun together."

Sammie would fold Flat Dog to carry around
in her pocket. She could hide him from everyone!

At mealtime, Sammie lay Flat Dog on her lap
and dropped tiny bits of food for him to eat.

At bedtime, Sammie tucked Flat Dog into
the pajama pocket closest to her heart.

At recess, Sammie ran around the playground so Flat Dog could exercise.

On windy days,
Flat Dog sometimes
slipped out of Sammie's
hand and floated away.
Sammie felt scared.
Would Flat Dog fly up to the
clouds and never return?
But eventually, Flat Dog would
float down to her backyard.
Sammie sighed with relief.

Another time, Flat Dog
blew away and landed in
the neighbor's tree.
That wasn't fun.

But then once, he flew away and landed
right back into Sammie's open hands.
A perfect landing.
A perfect dog.

Over time, Flat Dog became dirty,
faded, wrinkled, torn around the edges,
and just a little smelly!

"I know!" Sammie said, "I'll give Flat Dog a bath with me!"
Mama Stacy filled the tub with warm water and soap that smelled like
bubblegum. Sammie hid Flat Dog under a towel and when her mom left,
carefully unfolded him and gently placed him on the water.

"Doesn't this feel good?" Sammie asked giggling as Flat Dog was getting covered in bubbles. "Watch out, they'll tickle your nose!"

But soon, something was very, very wrong.

Flat Dog started falling apart. The more Sammie tried helping
Flat Dog, the more he dissolved in her bath water until nothing
was left but a million billion tiny pieces of soggy paper.

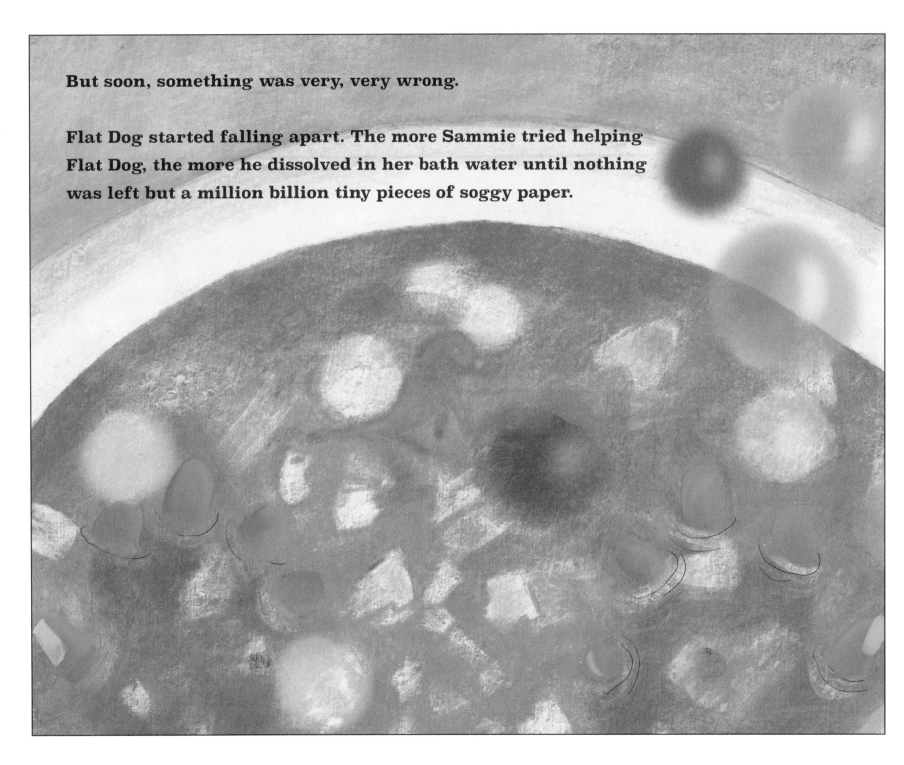

Mama Stacy could hear
Sammie crying. By the time
she came to see what was wrong,
Sammie was crying so hard
she couldn't speak.

Helping her out of the tub, Mama Stacy could see that Sammie was covered in a million billion tiny pieces of soggy paper. She carefully dried Sammie off, helped her into pajamas, and carried her to bed.

"You'll be okay," Mama Stacy said.

"Okay?" Sammie shouted inside her head. "Flat Dog is gone.
My best friend is gone! That's not okay!"

Mama Stacy and Mama Carla stood quietly in Sammie's bedroom doorway. They felt sad as they watched her toss, turn, and cry a bit before drifting off to sleep.

Sammie dreamed of Flat Dog eating ice cream with rainbow sprinkles, running around the playground, watching scary movies and floating in the sky.

Sammie reached into her pocket when she woke, but it was empty. She found the dog book filled with pictures and saw Flat Dog's missing page. She wanted her Flat Dog, but he was gone.

After breakfast, Mama Carla said they all needed to go to the store. Sammie didn't want to go but she was too young to stay at home alone.

They drove to a place she had never seen before
and went inside to meet a man who said
he had been waiting for them.

"Stay here, please," the man said as he left the room.
A few minutes later he returned. In his arms was a squirming puppy
with a waggly tail. "It's Flat Dog!" Sammie shouted.

"He's yours, honey," Mama Carla said as she carefully placed the puppy in Sammie's arms. "He's a rescue dog," Mama Stacy said. "A rescue dog is a dog that needs a new home and people who will love and take care of it."

Sammie laughed as Flat Dog licked her face.

"You proved how you could care for a pretend pet," Mama Carla said.

"We'll help you learn how to care for a real dog," she added.

"A real dog!" Sammie said with a big smile.

"He's so cute and wiggly, I think I'll call him Wiggles! Wiggles, the not-so-flat dog."

That night, Sammie and her family sat together eating ice cream with rainbow sprinkles and watched a not so scary movie. Sarah Jane was there, too.

Snugged in Sammie's lap instead of hiding in her pocket was her not-so-flat dog, Wiggles.

Sammie's heart was full of love.

"I love you Mama Stacy. I love you Mama Carla.
I love you Sarah Jane. I love you little Wiggles,"
she said as she hugged them one by one.

"This was the best day ever!"

# Find the Hidden Dogs!

I enjoyed working on this book so much I decided to add more fun for you! On each page I have hidden a dog for you to find. They are often one color, different sizes and blend in with their surroundings. I have included an enlargement of a page to show you what a hidden dog might look like.

If you can't find a hidden dog why not invite a friend or family member to help you.

Good luck and have fun!

Gary

# Enjoy these Fun Activities!

**Continuing the Story**

Encourage your child to talk about the story with these questions to develop empathy, problem solving skills, spark curiosity, and strengthen imagination:

• What did you like most about the Flat Dog story?
• When did the story make you feel happy?
• When did the story make you feel sad?
• What can you imagine Sammie and Wiggles doing together when they got home?

**Learning to Draw Flat Dog**

Invite your child to have fun drawing their own Flat Dog with these simple steps.

1. Draw an oval

2. Add two small ovals for ears

3. Draw two even smaller ovals for eyes

4. Add two small circles for pupils and lines for eyebrows

5. Add another circle for his nose and color!

# Thinking About Adopting a Pet?

Sammie wanted a dog more than anything else and practiced with Flat Dog to help her and her parents determine if they were ready for that commitment. During their research to find a dog for Sammie, her moms learned about "puppy mills," where dogs are bred quickly in unsafe conditions and often sold to pet supply stores. They also learned about the many wonderful dogs waiting in animal shelters for someone to give them a forever home.

When they were ready, Sammie and her family visited a pet adoption center. When you are ready to adopt a pet, after lots of conversation and thought, search online for **humane societies**, **animal shelters**, and **rescue groups** in your area that work to connect thousands of animals with loving homes every year. Many of these organizations vaccinate animals before adoption; they might also provide medical care, emergency response for animals in crisis, and advocacy for stronger laws to protect animals. National organizations, such as the American Society for the Prevention of Cruelty to Animals (ASPCA), also work to save animals and connect pets with loving homes.

Events such as "pet adoption days" hosted by animal shelters, rescue groups, and other organizations can be a helpful time to meet several adoption-ready pets when you are ready to adopt. Hopeful pet parents are asked to provide information about the family, home, and experience with pet parenting, so that animals are adopted into safe environments.